FOR THE TOYMAKERS OF OLD AND THE INNOCENCE OF PLAY. **B** **W**

TO CLAIRE, MY VERY OWN NINJA GIRL WHO'S KEPT THIS MEGABOT SANE AND HAPPY OVER THE YEARS. THANK YOU. :{> **B** **S** **W**

A Random House book

Published by Random House Australia Pty Ltd

Level 3, 100 Pacific Highway, North Sydney NSW 2060

www.randomhouse.com.au

First published by Random House Australia in 2011

Addresses for companies within the Random House Group can be found at www.randomhouse.com.au/offices

National Library of Australia Cataloguing-in-Publication entry

Author: Whatley, Bruce

Title: Tin Toys / Bruce Whatley; Ben Smith Whatley

ISBN: 978 1 86471 991 8 (hbk.)

ISBN: 978 1 86471 993 2 (pbk.)

Other contributors: Ben Smith Whatley

Dewey number: A823.3

Cover and internal design by Anna Bach

Typeset in Baskerville Greek Upright 16/22 by Anna Bach

Printed and bound in China by Midas Printing International Limited.

10 9 8 7 6 5 4 3 2 1

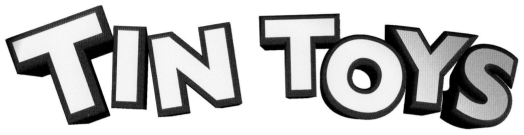

TIN TOYS

BRUCE WHATLEY

BEN SMITH WHATLEY

RANDOM HOUSE AUSTRALIA

As Christmas Eve approached, all the toys in the toyshop watched and waited. They chatted softly while the Shopkeeper slumbered in his chair. At the very back of the top shelf, the Space Ride gathered dust.

The new toys never noticed it as they weren't around for very long. They arrived just before Christmas with posters and sale tags and were gone by Christmas Eve.

But the older toys had not forgotten the Space Ride. Buster could remember the first time he saw it in action. It whirred and whizzed, ready for take-off. It was magnificent.

It was an old-fashioned wind-up toy, worked by a key inserted in a small hole between the words 'Space' and 'Ride'. But the key was long gone.

There were other wind-up toys with keys in the shop. Buster and Roy had tried Annie's pretty golden key, Chirpy Chick's small silver key, as well as the large black key from Salesman Sam and Doris Dial-up typewriter's tiny key. But none of them fitted.

'Oh, I wish you could see it!' said Buster. 'Stars! I'm talking solar systems! Galaxies! We just need the key.'

The new batch of toys didn't understand what all the fuss was about. They had bits that lit up – shiny new-age plastic bits. And some of them had appeared on TV and the big screen. They were movie stars!

Megabot was the largest of the new toys with the smallest sense of humour, and full of his own importance. The Space Ride sounded like a piece of junk to him.

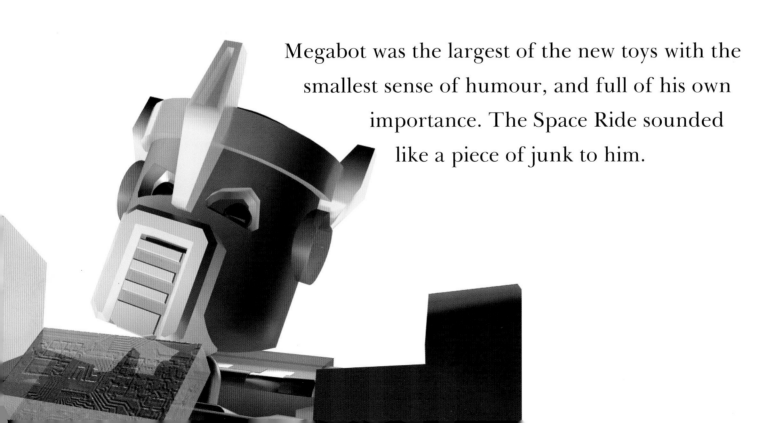

The only key Buster and Roy hadn't tried hung
from the watch chain on the Shopkeeper's waistcoat.
But how could they get it?

Buster had a plan and he needed the new toys to help.
Although they grumbled about it, they agreed.

'Galaxies, indeed!' said Megabot.

'Anything for a laugh,' said Teeth,
which was about all he could do really.

First they got down from the shelf.

Then they sneaked across the floor.

Climbed up the chair and reached for the key while Chirpy Chick created a diversion.

The plan worked perfectly until . . . the Shopkeeper looked down. Buster winked and shrugged. The Shopkeeper shrieked and ran for the door. He'd never had a toy wink and smile at him before.

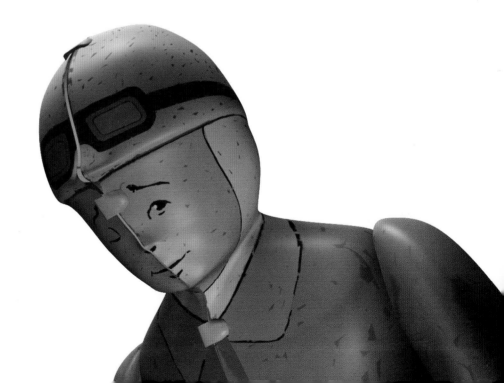

As the Shopkeeper tried to escape, Chirpy jumped for the key. And Megabot jumped for Chirpy.

'Oops,' said Megabot as he pulled off her leg by mistake.

On the back shelf, Christmas Eve was even quieter than usual.

Chirpy hadn't been seen since the Shopkeeper ran screaming out the door.

Click . . . Click . . . Click . . . Click . . .

'Chirpy!'

Megabot picked her up and handed back her leg. 'Sorry,' he whispered as he placed her gently back on the shelf, the key held firmly in her beak.

Buster took it from her and found the keyhole on the Space Ride.

The key fitted. He turned it and they all stepped back to watch.

S lowly the Space Ride lifted, rolled off the shelf and floated to the floor. And ever so slowly, it started to turn. Around and around! Around and around! Around and . . .

'Is that all it does?' asked Megabot.

'Yes, fantastic, isn't it?' said Buster.

But even he had to admit that it wasn't quite as earth-shattering as he remembered.

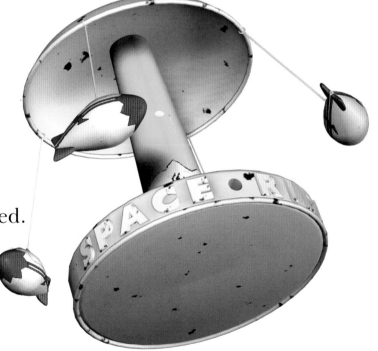

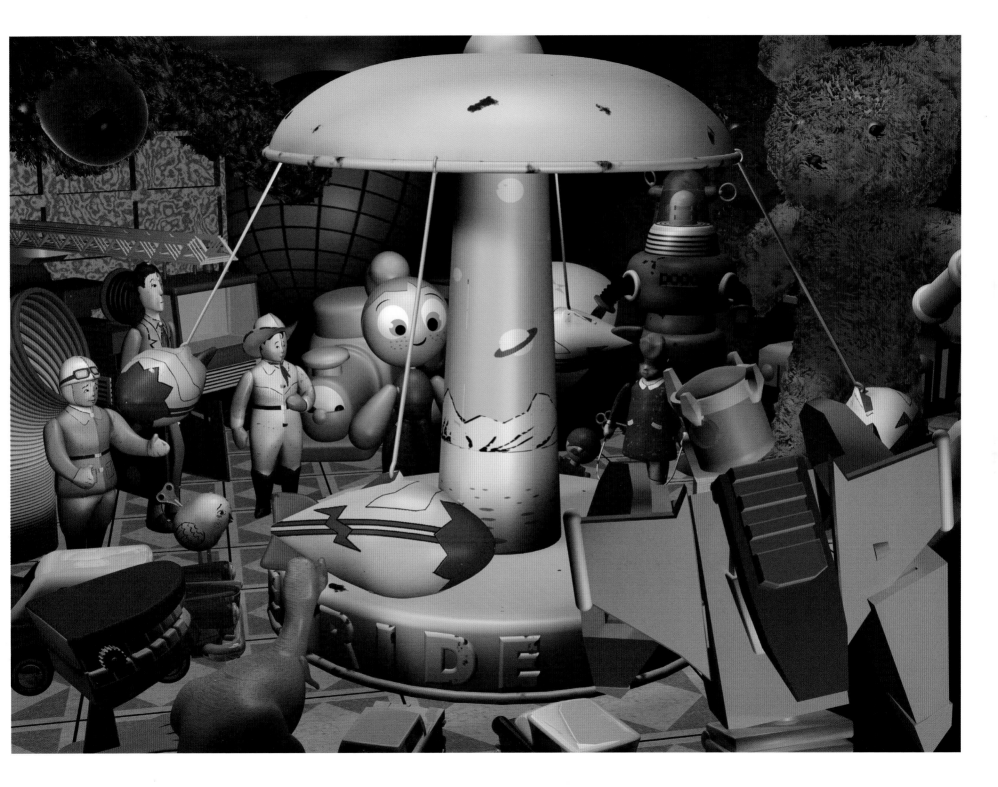

But then Teeth saw the funny side and started to laugh. Roy and Buster laughed. Megabot laughed too, and that was a surprise.

The toys jumped and slid, popped and rolled, twirled and chattered. And laughed and laughed and laughed.

I t was the best Christmas Eve ever.

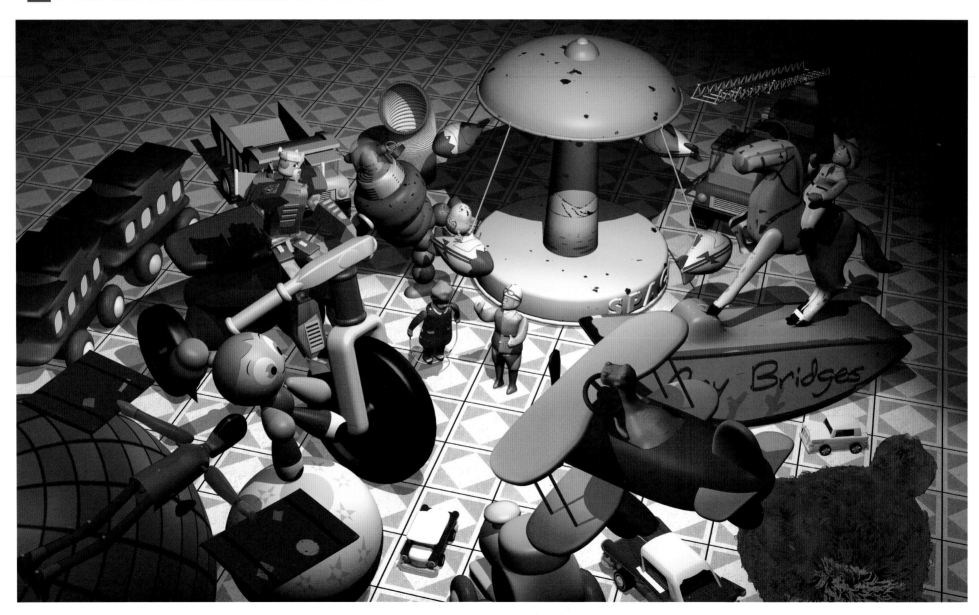